# THE
# GREEN
# WOMAN

VERTIGO
DC COMICS

# THE GREEN WOMAN

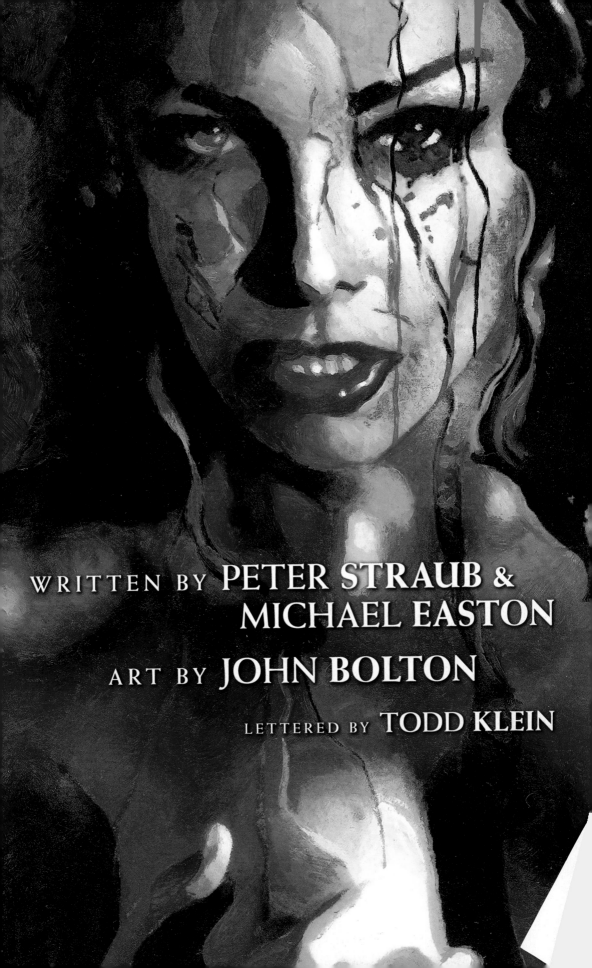

WRITTEN BY PETER STRAUB &
MICHAEL EASTON

ART BY JOHN BOLTON

LETTERED BY TODD KLEIN

*Dedications*

Peter Straub & Michael Easton
*For Robert S. Woods.*

John Bolton
*To my friend the actor
Peter Capaldi for being
the perfect villain.*

**Karen Berger** SVP-Executive Editor
**Jonathan Vankin** Editor
**Sarah Litt and Mark Doyle** Assistant Editors
**Robbin Brosterman** Design Director-Books
**Curtis King Jr.** Senior Art Director

DC COMICS
**Diane Nelson** President
**Dan DiDio and Jim Lee** Co-Publishers
**Geoff Johns** Chief Creative Officer
**Patrick Caldon** EVP-Finance and Administration
**John Rood** EVP-Sales, Marketing and Business Development
**Amy Genkins** SVP-Business and Legal Affairs
**Steve Rotterdam** SVP-Sales and Marketing
**John Cunningham** VP-Marketing
**Terri Cunningham** VP-Managing Editor
**Alison Gill** VP-Manufacturing
**David Hyde** VP-Publicity
**Sue Pohja** VP-Book Trade Sales
**Alysse Soll** VP-Advertising and Custom Publishing
**Bob Wayne** VP-Sales
**Mark Chiarello** Art Director

SUSTAINABLE
FORESTRY
INITIATIVE
Certified Chain of Custody
Promoting Sustainable
Forest Management
www.sfiprogram.org
Fiber used in this product line meets the
sourcing requirements of the SFI program.
www.sfiprogram.org SGS-SFI/COC-US10/81072

MAYBE YOU **KNOW** MY NAME.

YEAH, YOU MAY HAVE HEARD OF ME. GUY WROTE A **BOOK** ABOUT ME ONCE.

HE WANTED A NICE, PRETTY ENDING TO HIS STORY. HE THOUGHT IT WOULD PUT A LITTLE **BOW** ON TOP IF I GOT KILLED.

YEA THOUGH I WALK THROUGH THE VALLEY OF DEATH I AM NOT AFRAID FOR I AM THE EVILEST MOTHERFUCKER IN THE JUNGLE.

**WRITERS.** ISN'T A WRITER BORN WHO DOESN'T TURN INTO A LYING **PIECE OF SHIT** THE SECOND HE PICKS UP A PEN.

BEING GOOD WITH WORDS DOESN'T EXACTLY MAKE YOU A FUCKING VISIONARY, EITHER.

ALLOW ME TO INTRODUCE MYSELF. I'M **FIELDING BANDOLIER.** OF COURSE, OVER THE YEARS I HAD TO USE SOME **DIFFERENT** NAMES.

ACTUALLY, A **LOT** OF DIFFERENT NAMES.

WHEN I WAS A GREEN BERET, THEY CALLED ME FRANKLIN BACHELOR. WHEN I WAS A COP, THEY CALLED ME FRANK BELKNAP.

YOU GET CONFUSED, JUST CALL ME **FB**. A MAN LIKES TO HAVE A TRADEMARK.

MY WIFE SAW ALL OF ME. NAME WAS BEE, AND SHE SAW EVERYTHING. GODDAMN BEE SHOULD HAVE WRITTEN THE GODDAMN BOOK.

ME, I'M ONE OF THE ILLUMINATED ONES, AN *ILLUMINATI* OF THE GREEN WOMAN. ALWAYS FELT...WELL, *ORDAINED.*

THE *CORP,* THE *CIA,* WHOEVER THEY GOT, THEY'RE *NEVER* GONNA STOP ME. BUT, OH LORD, THEY HAVE TRIED.

DO YOU REALLY THINK SOME *AMATEUR* PRIVATE EYE WOULD'A HAD A SHOT?

ASSHOLE *WRITERS.*

TIME TO TURN THIS PISSHOLE *BEER* BACK INTO PISSHOLE *WATER.*

GODDAMMIT.

I WANTED YOU, *FRANK BELKNAP.*

*NO* ONE...EVER TOLD ME THEY *WANTED* ME.

13

I'VE BEEN A GOOD **SERVANT.**

BUT HAVEN'T I DONE **ENOUGH?** HAVEN'T I?

SLAM

New York City.

SHIT.

HOLY SHIT.

21

I PLANTED A **LOT** OF THINGS OUT HERE. NOT ALL OF THEM FLOWERS.

YOU COULD CALL THIS THE LAST ACT. HELL, YOU COULD CALL IT THE ENCORE, IT'S PRETTY MUCH THE SAME TO ME.

SWEET JESUS.

After Dark.

LADY, IF THERE'S ONE BITCH IN ALL THIS WORLD I **DON'T** WANT TO PISS OFF, IT'S YOU.

IN THE MIDDLE OF THE **NIGHT**, I HEAR THE SHIT YOU **WHISPER**.

PUSSY.

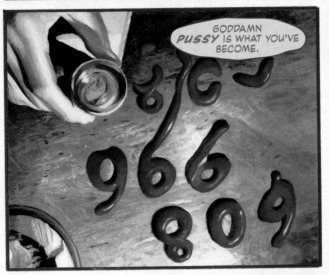

GODDAMN **PUSSY** IS WHAT YOU'VE BECOME.

The Voice From Underneath

**LOOK** AT YOURSELF, FEE. DICKLESS WONDER.

THE **OLD** YOU WOULD'VE BEEN ON THIS ALREADY.

31

34

THE "VIRGIN KILLER," HUH?

YOU CAN THANK *THE POST* FOR THAT ONE.

DON'T GET HIM *STARTED,* DOC.

TELL ME, DETECTIVE STEELE, DO YOU SEE ANY *SIGNIFICANCE* TO THE DRESSES?

THEY'RE MARRIED TO GOD NOW.

C'MON, ROLLO. WHAT KIND OF *GUINEA* ARE YOU, ANYWAY?

I WAS BORN IN POUGHKEEPSIE. WHATA'YOU *WANT* FROM ME? I HAD TO EXPLAIN TO EVERY TEACHER IN GRADE SCHOOL HOW TO *SPELL* MY NAME.

WELL, I LIVED ON *CARMINE STREET* FOR TEN YEARS AND *REAL* ITALIANS ARE VERY SPECIFIC ABOUT THIS KIND OF STUFF.

42

43

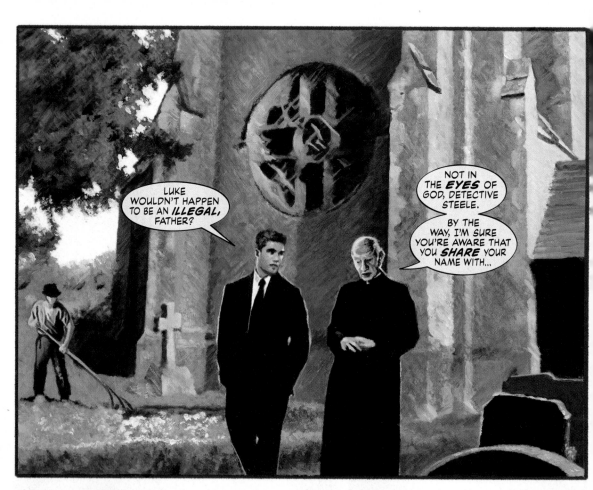

LUKE WOULDN'T HAPPEN TO BE AN *ILLEGAL*, FATHER?

NOT IN THE *EYES* OF GOD, DETECTIVE STEELE.

BY THE WAY, I'M SURE YOU'RE AWARE THAT YOU *SHARE* YOUR NAME WITH...

OF COURSE YOU ARE.

NOT MANY PEOPLE *REMEMBER* OL' BOB STEELE NOW, BUT IN MY DAY HE WAS A *GREAT HERO* TO ME.

ODD AS IT MAY SOUND FATHER, IN A SENSE, HE'S *ALWAYS* WITH ME.

THAT BASTARD WON'T LET ME FORGET THE STRING OF CASES THAT ROAR THROUGH MY SHATTERED NIGHTS, MY WRUNG OUT MORNINGS...

45

LOOK AT THAT WOMAN.
MY GOD, LOOK AT HER.

THUP

THUP

THUP

In the distant World beating behind all our thoughts...

**III Corps at Ho Ngoc Tau,** Project Sigma: Between Saigon and Long Binh. 1968.

**SAPPERS** IN THE WIRE! SAPPERS IN THE **WIRE!**

FOXFIRE, WE NEED AIR CAV-- **FOXFIRE,** DO YOU READ--

RADIO'S **DEAD,** SIR--

GOD **SAVE** US, SPANGLER. WHAT'S **YOUR** POSITION ON **MIRACLES?**

53

AND SOMETIMES--

--YOU JUST GOTTA GET *UP CLOSE* AND PERSONAL.

59

TRAGEDY **DOES** SEEM TO FOLLOW YOU **AROUND**, BACHELOR.

HOW **SO**, SIR?

FOR STARTERS, YOUR BIRTH MOTHER **DIED** WHEN YOU WERE A BABY.

AND YOUR FATHER WAS **MURDERED** THE LAST TIME YOU WERE BACK IN **CONUS**?

KILLER WAS NEVER **CAUGHT**, IS THAT RIGHT?

THIS MIGHT SOUND FUNNY TO A GOOD MAN LIKE **YOURSELF**, SIR...

...BUT I FIGURE MY DAD JUST GOT WHAT WAS **COMING** TO HIM.

ACCORDING TO THE **LORD**, ANYHOW.

WHAT MAKES YOU **SAY** THAT, PRIVATE?

SEEMS YOU ALREADY GOT THE **WHOLE** STORY IN YOUR **FILES**, SIR.

WE WANT TO HEAR IT FROM **YOU**, SOLDIER.

ONLY MOTHER I EVER **KNEW** WAS MY STEPMOTHER, AND HE BEAT THE **STUFFING** OUT OF HER ABOUT ONCE A WEEK.

SOUNDS PRETTY **GRIM**, TROOP.

**AFFIRMATIVE**, SIR. ONE NIGHT WHEN I WAS EIGHT, HE BEAT HER SO **BAD** SHE NEVER RECOVERED. PRETENDED SHE WAS **GOING** TO GET BETTER, BUT ALL SHE DID WAS ROT AWAY IN HER **BED**.

I WAS **WITH** HER WHEN SHE DIED.

I DON'T THINK WE NEED **DETAIN** YOU ANYMORE, BACHELOR.

THAT SPOOKY SON OF A **BITCH** IS **COMPLETELY** OFF THE CHARTS.

SO HOW DO WE GET **RID** OF HIM? DISCHARGE?

OH, HIM WE'RE **KEEPING**. CAN'T **WASTE** A SOLDIER LIKE THAT, MAJOR.

JUST GET HIM **OUT** OF THIS MAN'S ARMY, AND I'LL BE HAPPY.

HE'LL BE OUT OF **YOUR** ARMY. HE JUST **WON'T** BE OUT OF OURS.

WHAT DOES **THAT** MEAN?

YOU NEVER **HEARD** THIS, AND I NEVER **SAID** IT, BUT RIGHT AT THE TOP OF SPECIAL FORCES, WE HAVE AN ALL-VOLUNTEER PROJECT CALLED **MACV-SOG**.

MILITARY ADVISORY **COMMAND** VIETNAM STUDIES AND OBSERVATION **GROUP**. DON'T BELIEVE THE **NAME**, MAJOR. IT'S A HIGHLY **SECRET**, UNCONVENTIONAL WARFARE **TASK** FORCE.

YOU COULD SAY WE'RE GOING TO GIVE THIS **DEEPLY** MOTIVATED SOLDIER AN ARMY ALL HIS OWN.

THE **COMPANY** GOT A LOT OF BANG FOR ITS BUCK. WE KILLED TWENTY FOR EVERY ONE WE LOST. WE WERE THE SINGLE **MOST** COST-EFFECTIVE UNIT IN THE **ENTIRE** U.S. MILITARY.

SOME ARE LOST IN WAR. I **FOUND** MYSELF. I LIVED IN THE **REALM** OF GODS.

AFTER ALL THAT TROUBLE, ALL THAT **CRAZINESS**, I WAS FINALLY **HOME.**

I WAS **FREE.** I WAS **MYSELF.**

I WON'T HURT **HER.** NOT **THIS** ONE.

HOW COULD I KILL **ANYTHING** SO LOVELY? AFTER ALL, SHE MIGHT AS WELL BE MY **WIFE.**

AND THOSE **EYES.**

THOSE BEAUTIFUL ALMOND-COLOR EYES. LIKE CAVES YOU COULD GET LOST IN.

GOT TO HAND IT TO YOU, OLD MAN. YOU HAVE **EXQUISITE** TASTE.

LAY A HAND ON HER, BILLY, AND I'LL BEAT YOU BLIND.

OKAY, OKAY. IT'S JUST, YOU KNOW THE RULES, POPS. **DALLY** TOO LONG AND I'LL HAVE TO GET IN THERE.

WHO'S THERE?

MOVE OVER ROVER, LET **BILLY** TAKE OVER.

YOU MUST BE **FRANK.**

THEY BUILT THE PLACE USING TIMBERS FROM A **SHIP** ON WHICH THE CREW ALL WENT CRAZY AND **KILLED** EACH OTHER. THAT'S HOW IT GOT ITS **NAME**.

GUESS THE **WOOD** WENT CHEAP.

THANKS TO YOUR **ILLEGAL** SEARCH, NONE OF THAT'S ADMISSABLE NOW.

THAT PUNK LUKE, HE'S THE **VIRGIN KILLER**.

EXACTLY. A **DREAM**. NIGHTMARE, **WHATEVER** YOU WANT TO CALL IT. AND **THAT** PIECE OF **SHIT** WAS IN IT.

SWEET JESUS, DON'T TELL ME. ANOTHER **VISION**, BOBBY? HOLY **CRAP**--

LOOK AT WHAT ELSE I FOUND AT HIS PLACE. FUCKIN' **POLICE** FILES. AUTOPSY REPORTS. **FORENSIC** PHOTOS.

LITTLE **PRICK** WAS IN LOVE WITH THIS GUY IN THE **MIDWEST** THEY DUBBED "THE **BIRTHDAY KILLER**."

EVIDENCE

ANOTHER ONE THEY CALLED THE **HIGHWAY KILLER**. MAKES ME THINK, MAYBE THEY WERE THE **SAME** GUY.

IT'S SICK, BUT I'VE SEEN IT BEFORE, BOBBY. HELL, PEOPLE COLLECT **NAZI** CRAP, DOESN'T MAKE 'EM **HIMMLER**.

HE'S GOT A FUCKIN' "**HOW TO**" MANUAL HERE. HE GETS **OFF** ON IT. LIKE **HERO** WORSHIP SHIT.

Betty Powell

CARDINAL EGAN *HIMSELF* IS LUKE'S ALIBI FOR AT LEAST ONE OF THE MURDERS.

*IAD* IS SCARED SHITLESS OF A LAWSUIT. THEY'VE ALREADY BEGUN *PROCESSING* HIM FOR RELEASE.

TAKING THESE FILES WITH ME. DON'T SAY ANYTHING TO THE CAPTAIN.

AND GET SOMETHING FOR THAT ITCH, ROLLO.

WHERE ARE YOU *GOING,* BOBBY?

*FISHING.* TAKE *CARE* OF YOURSELF.

YOU TOO, *BUDDY BOY.*

NAME'S *ROMAN GARKO.* I WANT TO TALK TO STEELE, *NOW.*

*IAD* NEEDS TO WORK ON THEIR *TIMING.* FOR ONE THING, BOBBY'S OFF *FISHING.* FOR ANOTHER, I THINK HE JUST WALKED *AWAY* FROM THIS CRAPPY JOB.

YEAH, THIS *ALIQUIPPA* P.D.? SERGEANT *WOODS?*

YOU THE GUY THAT'S BEEN CALLING ABOUT BETTY *POWELL?* SURE, I REMEMBER. NEVER SEEN ONE *CUT UP* LIKE THAT BEFORE. OR SINCE.

GUY WAS A LITERAL *KILLING* MACHINE.

FREDDY *BALSAM* WAS THE *BEST* HOMICIDE DETECTIVE WE EVER SAW IN *MANSFIELD.* HELL, IN ALL OF *OHIO.* A REAL *MASTER* OF HIS CRAFT.

OF COURSE, YOU COULD SAY THE *SAME* THING ABOUT THE *BIRTHDAY KILLER.* NOW LET ME *THINK.* WHO WERE HIS FIRST VICTIMS?

SHIRLEY HOPE. MARJORIE PACKER.

YOU KNOW YOUR *STUFF,* DETECTIVE. I'LL GIVE YOU THAT.

YEAH, *A.D.A. DEL,* I GOT *THAT* GOING FOR ME.

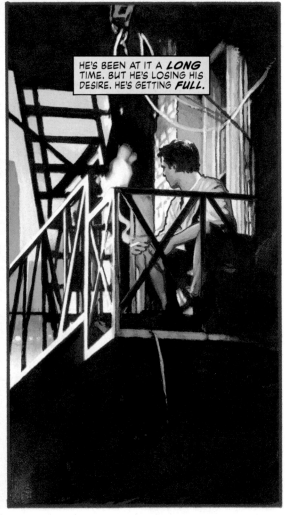

HE'S BEEN AT IT A *LONG* TIME. BUT HE'S LOSING HIS DESIRE. HE'S GETTING *FULL.*

WHAT WAS HIS *NAME* AGAIN, DETECTIVE HENDERSON?

REAL *CRACKER-JACK* INVESTIGATOR, TOO. THINK HE WAS *SPECIAL FORCES* IN 'NAM.

BELKNAP. FRANKIE *BELKNAP*. IT BROKE THAT BOY'S *HEART* HE COULD NEVER SOLVE THAT *HIGHWAY KILLER* BUSINESS. HE LEFT THE FORCE BECAUSE OF THAT CASE.

COULD'A SWORE I SAW *SOMETHING* ABOUT BELKNAP SOMEWHERE...

BOB *STEELE* YOUR REAL NAME, KID? HEY, WHO WAS STEELE'S BIG RIVAL IN THE MOVIES?

UH, KEN *MAYNARD*.

*MAYNARD*. YEAH. YOU KNOW, I USED TO THINK *BELKNAP* LOOKED A LITTLE LIKE MAYNARD.

I HEARD BELKNAP STOPPED A BULLET IN HIS NEXT JOB. HELL OF A LOSS.

I REMEMBER HIS *FACE* LIKE IT WAS YESTERDAY. KILLER SMILE. FRANKIE HAD THOSE *DEAD LEVEL* EYES YOU NEVER FORGET.

BELKNAP

Millhaven League
Birthday Killer Claims Four Victim

70

HI, *HONEY. I'M HOME.*

I FEEL LIKE THE **WHOLE WORLD'S** GOING TO SHIT.

BABY, THE WAY YOU **FEEL** IS WHAT TURNS ME **ON** ABOUT YOU.

KNOCK
KNOCK

WHO
IS IT?

DRY-
CLEANING.

OH. WHAT
HAPPENED TO
*JIMMY?*

JIMMY'S
OUT SICK, MA'AM.
TERRIBLE *HEAD
COLD.* I'M
*BILLY.*

THANK
YOU, BILLY. OH,
WAIT...

NOT
NECESSARY,
MA'AM. JUST
SEEING YOUR
*PRETTY FACE*
IS GRATUITY
ENOUGH.

HAVE A NICE
EVENING.

IT'S BEEN A LONG TIME SINCE SOMEONE'S ASKED ME OUT, FRANK.

I FEEL LIKE EVERYONE IS *LOOKING* AT US.

YOU'RE SO BEAUTIFUL. I'M *OLD* ENOUGH TO BE YOUR...

YOU REMIND ME OF MY UNCLE LEE. HE WAS A *SOLDIER* IN MAO'S ARMY. HE RAISED ME AFTER MY *PARENTS* DIED.

I *LIKE* OLDER MEN. WHO WANTS TO GO OUT WITH *BOYS?*

THERE'S SOME STUFF YOU OUGHT TO *KNOW* ABOUT ME, TOO.

A LONG *TIME* AGO, WHEN I WAS IN THE SPECIAL FORCES, I WAS *MARRIED* TO A MONTAGNYARD WOMAN, HER NAME WAS *BEE.*

A RHADE, THE DAUGHTER OF THE LOCAL **CHIEF.** I LOVED HER--LOVED **EVERYTHING** ABOUT HER.

THE ARMY DIDN'T **LIKE** MY MARRIAGE, BUT I HAD AN OUTSTANDING **RECORD** AND THEY DIDN'T WANT TO **MESS** WITH ME...

YOU MIGHT NOT GUESS IT, BUT I HAD A **REPUTATION** OVER THERE...

I COULD **TELL** THAT YOU WERE A MAN OF GREAT **EXPERI-ENCE.**

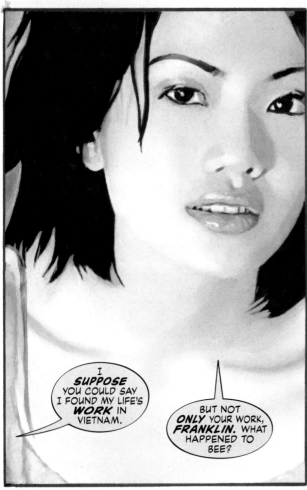

I **SUPPOSE** YOU COULD SAY I FOUND MY LIFE'S **WORK** IN VIETNAM.

BUT NOT **ONLY** YOUR WORK, **FRANKLIN.** WHAT HAPPENED TO BEE?

WHEN SHE WAS **KILLED,** WE'D BEEN MARRIED ONLY **EIGHT** MONTHS.

YOU ARE A **STRONG** AND **SENSITIVE** MAN, AND ALL YOUR EXPERIENCES HAVE ENRICHED YOU.

I'M JUST AN OL' RETIRED **WARRIOR.**

**TRUE** WARRIORS **NEVER** RETIRE, FRANK. THIS WAS WRITTEN **MANY** TIMES IN MY UNCLE LEE'S JOURNAL.

IT IS **WRITTEN.** THEY **FADE** AWAY, BUT IT TAKES A LONG, LONG **TIME.**

LONGER THAN **MOST** PEOPLE EVER LIVE.

FADING AWAY? THAT WAS MY **SPECIALTY.**

79

WHEN I RAN MY CAMP IN CAMBODIA, THEY CALLED ME "THE LAST IRREGULAR." THE LAST OFFICER ALLOWED TO INVENT THE WORLD THE WAY HE WANTED IT TO BE. AFTER ME, THEY THOUGHT THEY'D BETTER TIGHTEN UP THE PROTOCOLS.

‹THESE ARE OUR LAST DAYS. THEY HAVE BEEN GLORIOUS, MY HUSBAND. WE HAVE SEEN THE DARK FIRE AT THE CENTER OF LIFE.›

‹YOU HAVE TAKEN ME FAR FROM MY CENTRAL HIGHLANDS, BUT NOW YOU MUST GO ON ALONE.›

‹THOSE WHITE DEVILS, THEY SEARCH AND SEARCH, TO DRAG YOU BACK TO YOUR COUNTRY.›

‹I KNOW. WITH ALL MY HEART, I WISH THAT YOU COULD COME WITH ME, MY LOVE...›

‹BUT BECAUSE I CANNOT, I HAVE THE HONOR OF DYING BY YOUR HAND.›

‹THE SACRED KNIFE THAT ENTERS YOU IS ME.›

‹AND YOU WILL TAKE PART OF BEE ALWAYS WITH YOU.›

ALWAYS.

THE SACRED PATTERN HAD BEEN SET.

"UNCLE LEE KNEW MUCH *VIOLENCE* IN HIS LIFE..."

Belfast.
Northern
Ireland.

SON OF
A BITCH.

91

96

O MY BACKWARD ILL-TRAINED HEART...

Allentown, Pennsylvania 1973.

FOR TONIGHT'S LATE NIGHT MADNESS MASTERPIECE WE PRESENT 1944'S *TRIGGER LAW,* STARRING *BOB STEELE*--

--GREATEST OF ALL UNKNOWN COWBOY HEROES BACK IN THE DAY...

AND *HE'S GOING* TO COME FOR YOU, *FEE.*

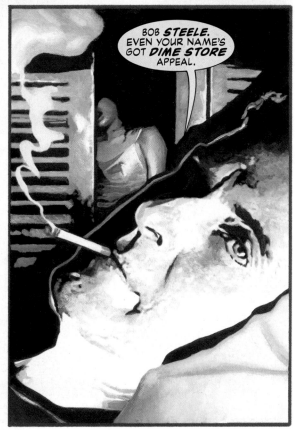

BOB *STEELE.* EVEN YOUR NAME'S GOT *DIME STORE* APPEAL.

101

Bee, I saw you in her. Your bones moved in my head my heart my terrible life. it was FOR YOU I sought her out not for me as I thought. surely your dead face smiled at your warrior. surely your dead hand caressed him. the dark fire draws very near, Bee, I feel the farthest edge of its warmth even now

Ulster County.
Upstate New York.

SCARED ME THERE FOR A *MOMENT,* FELLA.

Six months ago...

ADMIT IT, BUDDY BOY, YOU *DRANK* HEAVILY ALL THAT WEEK.

WE'RE *NOT* BUDDIES, STOP CALLING ME *BUDDY BOY.*

I *DON'T* THINK YOU *HAVE* ANY BUDDIES, DO YOU, STEELE?

NOT IF YOU DON'T COUNT YOUR *MOTHER* AND THAT *GIRL SCOUT* TROOP.

*OKAY,* THEN. WHEN YOU WERE IN *BELFAST* ON YOUR *MAD DOG* MISSION, HOW MANY DRINKS WOULD YOU SAY YOU TOOK ON AN *AVERAGE* DAY?

I *WASN'T* COUNTING.

SO LET'S SAY, AN AVERAGE OF *TEN* DRINKS A DAY.

SAY WHATEVER YOU WANT, GARKO. BUT TEN DRINKS A DAY AIN'T SHIT IN BELFAST.

ONE NIGHT I SAW AN OLD *SHIPBUILDER* PUT AWAY EIGHTEEN STRAIGHT *WHISKIES,* ONE RIGHT AFTER THE OTHER. THE GUY LOOKED LIKE HE COULD HAVE RIPPED *GIRDERS* IN HALF WITH HIS BARE HANDS.

LET'S GET *BACK* TO THE SUBJECT AT HAND...

THAT *IS* THE SUBJECT AT HAND. HAVE YOU HEARD OF THE GOOD SHIP *BONIFACE,* COMMONLY KNOWN AS THE BLACK GALLEON?

ONLY FROM *YOU,* BUDDY BOY.

I THINK IT MADE THE WHOLE *CREW* COMMIT MASS *MURDER...*

THE SHIP *MADE* THE CREW KILL EACH OTHER?

...EVIL *COMES* IN MANY FORMS, *GARKO.*

SO *YOU* SAY, DETECTIVE.

DO YOU STILL *BELIEVE,* DESPITE HAVING BEEN *SODDEN* WITH ALCOHOL AND SUBJECT TO *DELUSIONS,* THAT YOU SHOT AND *KILLED* YOUR SUSPECT?

I SHOT AT SOMETHING. COULD IT HAVE BEEN THAT *MURDEROUS* ASSHOLE? YEAH, WHY NOT?

EVEN THOUGH NO *BODY PARTS* WERE FOUND IN THE REMAINS OF THE FIRE. NO RECOGNIZABLE *HUMAN* BODY PARTS, ANYHOW. *SOME* OF THAT STUFF, WELL...

THAT WAS THE *ASSHOLE.* TAKE MY WORD FOR IT.

WHEN YOU WERE QUESTIONED IN *IRELAND,* YOU SAID THAT AT THE MOMENT YOU FIRED YOUR *WEAPON,* "A STRANGE *FORCE* SEEMED TO PENETRATE" YOUR SKIN?

*EXACTLY.* SKIN-PENETRATION, A *WHOLE BODY* EXPERIENCE.

UH *HUH.* AND THIS *FORCE* RAN THROUGHOUT YOU LIKE "AN ELECTRIC *CURRENT* THAT *PIERCED* YOUR HEART AND YOUR LUNGS," VIRTU-ALLY *CRIPPLING* YOU.

YES...BUT YOU KNOW, I NEVER SAID *ANYTHING* ABOUT THE HEADLESS CORPSES FLOATING IN THE *SEA OF BLOOD.*

YOU SURE IT WASN'T A *RIVER OF WHISKEY,* DETECTIVE? OR PERHAPS A MOUND OF COLOMBIAN MARCHING POWDER?

GO TO *HELL,* GARKO.

THE *FIGUREHEAD* OF *THAT* SHIP WENT TO AMERICA. NO ONE KNOWS *WHERE.* WOULDN'T YOU LIKE TO *FIND* IT?

I'D LIKE TO *KNOW* IF IT *SAYS* THINGS AT NIGHT. I'D LIKE TO KNOW *WHO* IT TALKS TO, WOULDN'T YOU?

VERY *CUTE,* DETECTIVE STEELE. YOU REALLY *EXPECT* ME TO BELIEVE *ANY* OF THIS?

I DON'T GIVE A *DAMN* IF YOU DO OR NOT, AGENT GARKO.

OH, BUT I THINK YOU *DO.* I THINK YOU WANT TO COME OUT OF THIS A *HERO.* I THINK YOU WANT TO KEEP GETTING YOUR *PENSION.* PLUS *DISABILITY.*

YOU WANT THE *DEPARTMENT* TO PAY FOR ALL THOSE PILLS YOU POP. AND WHY SHOULD YOU GET THIS *FREE RIDE?* ALL BECAUSE YOU CLAIM YOU SAW THE *BOGEY* MAN.

THE ONLY *EVIL* I SEE IN HERE DETECTIVE...IS *YOU.*

FIND A *LAWYER,* STEELE. YOU'RE GOING TO *NEED* ONE.

BRIING! BRIING!

THE ONE YOU SAID WAS A **COP.** WE HAD THIS **HOMICIDE,** MAN, AND I JUST HAD A FEELING... RIGHT AGE, **FEMALE,** CHINESE WOMAN WHO OWNED A **FLOWER** SHOP.

A LOT OF **KNIFE** WORK ON HER...JUST LIKE THOSE OLD **UN-SOLVEDS** YOU DUG UP ALL OVER THE COUNTRY.

BUDDY, YOU STILL **THERE?** MAYBE I SAID ENOUGH?

TO HELL WITH **YOU.** I DON'T **WANT** TO KNOW.

WHERE YOU AT THESE DAYS?

WELL, IF YOU **EVER** PICKED UP YOUR PHONE, YOU'D KNOW ABOUT THREE MONTHS AGO I TOOK MY **TWENTY-FIVE** AND GOT OUT. DOING SOME CONSULTING NOW WITH A LITTLE DEPARTMENT IN **MILLHAVEN,** ILLINOIS. **HELL** OF A NICE PLACE.

MILLHAVEN? YOU EVER HEAR ANYTHING ABOUT A COP NAMED **FRANK BELKNAP?**

ONLY THAT HE'S **DEAD.** OF COURSE, YOU WOULDN'T KNOW IT FROM THE WAY THEY TALK ABOUT HIM ALL THE TIME. KIND OF A **HERO** AROUND HERE.

HIS OLD PARTNER **HENDERSON** IS THE ONE WHO BROUGHT ME DOWN HERE. HE CALLED FOR YOU A COUPLE OF TIMES, THEY GOT ME **INSTEAD.**

IT'S OKAY TO BE **AFRAID** OF WHAT WE GOT OUT HERE, BOBBY. I KNOW SIX MONTHS AGO, YOU WOULD'A **JUMPED** AT THE CHANCE.

116

HOLY FUCKIN' *MAIRZY* DOATES.

FEMALE, *ASIAN*... AGE THIRTY-FIVE... PRELIMINARY BLOOD MATCH TO SAMPLE TAKEN FROM LOCAL *FLOWER* SHOP.

REPORTED MISSING APPROXIMATELY TEN WEEKS... LAB AND DENTAL PENDING.

SEVERAL *ORGANS* REMOVED, INCLUDING *SPLEEN*. INTRICATE *INCISION*, AVOIDANCE OF HEAVY BONE...DISPLAYING *SOME* KNOWLEDGE OF ANATOMY.

FAX

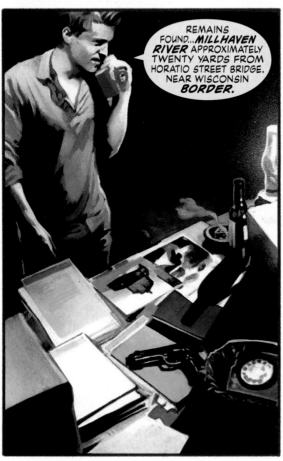

REMAINS FOUND...*MILLHAVEN RIVER* APPROXIMATELY TWENTY YARDS FROM HORATIO STREET BRIDGE, NEAR WISCONSIN *BORDER*.

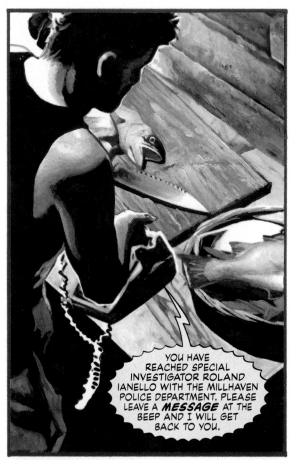

YOU HAVE REACHED SPECIAL INVESTIGATOR ROLAND IANELLO WITH THE MILLHAVEN POLICE DEPARTMENT. PLEASE LEAVE A *MESSAGE* AT THE BEEP AND I WILL GET BACK TO YOU.

HEY, ROLLO. IF THE *INVITATION'S* STILL OPEN, I *WILL* COME DOWN AND GIVE YOU AN ASSIST. I'D LIKE TO SEE WHERE THEY PULLED THE *GIRL* OUT OF THE RIVER.

AND IF *BELKNAP* SHOWS UP, GET THE HELL *OUT* OF THERE.

YOU *ARE* BOB *STEELE*, YOU *ARE*. IN SPITE OF *EVERYTHING*.

I'M *NOT* TALKING TO YOU.

125

126

129

F.B....

HE'S IN SO *DEEP* HE PROBABLY EVEN *SMELLS* LIKE BLOOD.

New York. Present day.

LIKE A HUNGRY *GHOST*. GHOSTS ARE *ALWAYS* HUNGRY.

THING IS, HE *CARES* ABOUT WHO HE KILLS. THIS GUY'S STILL A *SOLDIER*.

ONLY NOW, HE'S IN THAT *OTHER* ARMY.

131

133

SMASH!

FOUND HER CAR **ABANDONED** ABOUT FIVE KLICKS DOWNSTREAM. THEY PULLED HER OUT, WHAT WAS **LEFT** OF HER, WHERE THAT MARKER IS.

STILL **WAITING** ON THE LABS.

WHAT'S THAT PLACE?

**THAT?** IT'S AN OLD PUB. BEEN BOARDED UP FOR YEARS.

THIS WHOLE AREA'S GOT A **SCARY** FREAKIN' HISTORY, BUDDY. LOTTA YEARS AGO SOME STREETWALKER WAS **CHOPPED UP** BY HER HUSBAND RIGHT AROUND HERE. **CRAZY** SHIT ABOUT THE BAR-- HUNDRED YEARS AGO IT WAS BAD GUY **CENTRAL.**

YOU EVER BEEN **INSIDE** IT?

SOMEONE REPORTED SEEING A LIGHT ON INSIDE ONCE. A COUPLE OF UNITS CHECKED IT OUT. *NOTHING*.

PROBABLY SOME *KIDS* SMOKING DOPE. BEEN SEALED UP EVER SINCE.

NOTICE YOU DON'T *ITCH* SO MUCH ANYMORE.

AH, *BULLSHIT*. USING THIS CHINESE *GEL* ON IT. STINKS LIKE HELL.

GETTING OLD'S A *BITCH*, BOBBY.

JUST AN OLD FUCK NOW.

THERE'S NO *FUCK* LIKE AN OLD FUCK.

MISSED YOU, KID.

SAME *HERE*, ROLLO.

C'MON. I'LL DROP YOU AT YOUR HOTEL. YOU CAN RAID THE MINI BAR ON THE *CITY'S* DIME.

SO I'M WAITING ON THE **FEDS** TO GET BACK TO ME.

I'M IN OVER MY **HEAD** ON THIS ONE, AREN'T I, BUDDY?

YOU SURE AS **HELL** ARE.

SHIT. I BROUGHT YOU DOWN HERE TO SHINE A LITTLE LIGHT ON THE SITUATION, NOT SQUASH WHAT **PITIFUL** CONFIDENCE I HAVE LEFT IN ME.

YOU KNOW, I HADN'T SEEN THE OLD MAN FOR A LOT OF **YEARS** WHEN HE SHOWED UP FOR MY GRADUATION DAY FROM THE **ACADEMY.**

"IF YOU BRING FORTH WHAT'S **WITHIN** YOU, WHAT'S WITHIN YOU WILL **SAVE** YOU; IF YOU **DO NOT** BRING FORTH WHAT'S WITHIN YOU, WHAT YOU DO NOT BRING FORTH WILL **DESTROY** YOU."

THAT'S WHAT HE SAID TO ME AFTER THE **CEREMONY.** AND THEN HE WAS GONE. DIDN'T EVEN STICK AROUND LONG ENOUGH FOR THEM TO **CRACK** THE CHAMPAGNE. I THINK THAT'S THE ONLY **ADVICE** HE EVER GAVE ME...

I'M TOO FUCKED UP TO UNDERSTAND **ANY** OF THAT. I GOTTA GET HOME, BUD.

YOU EVER *TALK* TO YOUR DAD NOW? HE STILL KICKING AROUND?

HE'S *STILL* OUT THERE. LIKE THIS GUY WE'RE AFTER, HE'S TOO *MEAN* TO DIE.

I'LL PICK YOU UP IN THE MORNING.

*NIGHT,* ROLLO.

...I WASN'T EXPECTING AN ANSWERING MACHINE...WHEN DID YOU GET *THAT?* I KNOW IT'S BEEN A LONG TIME. I WAS...I WAS WATCHING THE RODEO ON TV AND I REMEMBERED HOW WE'D WATCH 'EM TOGETHER SOMETIMES...

...I REMEMBER HOW MOM WAS ALWAYS *WORRIED* ABOUT ME, YOU KNOW, ENDING UP ALONE, AND WHAT NOT. I WISH I COULD TELL HER THAT I FOUND SOMEONE. SHE'S A GOOD GIRL...HER NAME IS *JULES.* MIGHT EVEN GET MARRIED.

ANYWAY DAD, I KNOW THE MACHINE'S GONNA CUT ME OFF HERE, BUT I WANTED YOU TO KNOW I *UNDER-STAND* BETTER NOW. I'M SORRY I LET YOU DOWN. MAYBE SOMEDAY I'LL DO *SOMETHING* YOU CAN BE PROUD OF...

SOFT NOSED CARTR

LITTLE CLOWN, ARSONIST, MURDERER, YOU SHOULD HAVE STAYED AWAY. BUT YOU COULDN'T DO THAT, COULD YOU?

145

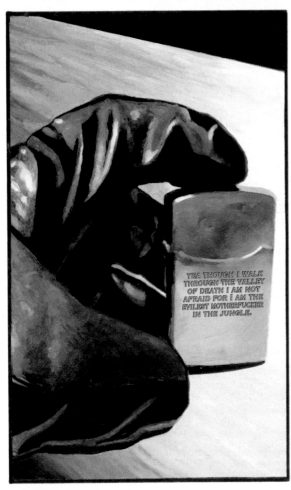

YEA THOUGH I WALK THROUGH THE VALLEY OF DEATH I AM NOT AFRAID FOR I AM THE EVILEST MOTHERFUCKER IN THE JUNGLE.

MAYBE YOU *KNOW* MY NAME...

The End

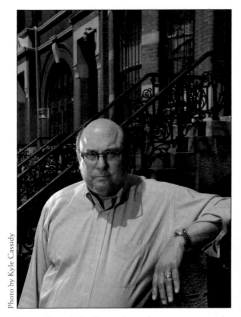

**Peter Straub** is the author of seventeen novels, which have been translated into more than twenty languages. They include *Ghost Story, Koko, Mr. X, In the Night Room*, and two collaborations with Stephen King, *The Talisman* and *Black House*. He has written two volumes of poetry and two collections of short fiction, and he edited the Library of America's edition of H. P. Lovecraft's *Tales* and the forthcoming Library of America's 2-volume anthology *American Fantastic Tales*. He has won the British Fantasy Award, eight Bram Stoker Awards, two International Horror Guild Awards, and two World Fantasy Awards. In 1998, he was named Grand Master at the World Horror Convention. In 2006, he was given the Horror Writers Association's Life Achievement Award. In 2008, he was given the Barnes & Noble Writers for Writers Award by Poets & Writers.

**Michael Easton** is the author of the critically acclaimed graphic novel trilogy *Soul Stealer* as well as the collection of poetry *Eighteen Straight Whiskeys*. He lives in New York.

**John Bolton** was seven when he first encountered a paint brush and it was love at first sight, offering him an outlet to visualize and create what he saw in his mind and put it to paper. Thus began a lifelong mission of creativity, with influences acquired from a wide variety of sources, but all connected by one underlying theme — the interesting and bizarre.

John has been painting professionally for three decades. His painting displays a thorough understanding of each medium and subject he chooses to tackle, horror being one of his favorites. John has collaborated with some of the industry's most prestigious comic writers, including Neil Gaiman, Mike Carey and Mark Verheiden. In the film world he has worked with Robert Zemeckis, Sam Raimi and Jonathan Glazer. He lives and works in London, England.